CAMEMBERT
and the
Magic Lamp

Lesley Young

Illustrated by José Ramón Sánchez

OCTOPUS

First published 1979 by
Octopus Books Limited
59 Grosvenor Street
London W1

Illustrations © 1978 Ediciones Altea, Madrid
This edition © 1979 Octopus Books Limited

Produced by Mandarin Publishers Ltd
22a Westlands Road, Quarry Bay,
Hong Kong

Printed in Singapore

ISBN 0 7064 1043 2

Contents

Chapter One
AT THE POST OFFICE

Camembert the mouse was working at the Post Office. He was a mouse to whom exciting things were always happening, but it looked as if he was going through a bad patch. His job was so boring! His nose was never out of forms, and his tongue was like sandpaper from licking piles of stamps.

Of course, he should leave the Post Office and find a job he would enjoy—like his Swiss uncle who put the holes in Emmental cheese. But he had a friend in the Post Office called Reginald, whom he didn't want to leave. He felt sorry for Reginald, who seemed to lead a very boring life. Camembert was sure that if he stayed around long enough, an adventure was bound to happen,

and he would make sure that Reginald was in on it.

At first Camembert had been a bit wary of Reginald. Perhaps he was one of those people who were frightened of mice. So for his first few days at the Post Office Camembert folded back his whiskers and tried to keep out of sight. But one day, at lunchtime, his nose began to twitch at the smell of cheese sandwiches, and Reginald looked over and spotted him. Thankfully, instead of screaming and jumping on his stool, he had smiled and offered Camembert a bit of his sandwich. Since then, he had often shared his lunch with Camembert, and the two became firm friends.

Camembert, in turn, helped Reginald by sharpening his pencils and sticking on stamps for him. He emptied his wastepaper basket by pushing the rubbish into an old mouse-hole he had found.

Camembert soon became used to the office routine and became a great help to Reginald. Thanks to him, Reginald could have forty winks after the morning tea break. On

winter mornings Camembert would sit in Reginald's cupped hand for warmth. So they found lots of ways in which they could help each other.

The other workers in the Post Office were astonished at Camembert's quick progress.

But when Camembert began to deal with the public, a few problems cropped up. A lady who was sending a parcel to her sister, became almost hysterical when a mouse arrived to stamp it!

'What are things coming to, when mice are working in the public services?' she screeched in alarm, rushing out with the parcel under her arm.

But most people took Camembert in their stride. After all, he was very polite and helpful—and more efficient than most of the others.

So Camembert became quite used to the work. He didn't care if the others pulled one of his legs from time to time. Little Miss Cooper, who

was in charge of Air Mail, was always going on about her lovely big tom cat. But she never brought him in, thank goodness! And old Smith kept bragging that he had the finest canaries in the City. So why shouldn't Reginald have a mouse for company? Not just any mouse of course, but a mouse who could speak several languages and was well-travelled, sophisticated and full of *joie de vivre*.

One day Reginald plucked up his courage and suggested to the Head of the Post Office that Camembert should be made an official employee.

Camembert soon learned to type and it was amazing to watch him speeding through his memos. Of course, there was no mouse-size typewriter in the office, but he jumped from key to key. Sometimes the whole staff would stop to watch him springing about as if he was on a trampoline.

Reginald encouraged his friend. But Camembert was not really ambitious—he only wanted to earn enough to keep himself in cheese.

How to make Typewriter Drawings

You can make lots of interesting pictures with the letters, dots and other symbols on a typewriter.

Make a simple geometric design—or something much more ambitious, like a poem about a cloud in the shape of a cloud!

If the drawing is complicated (like the portrait of Camembert on the page opposite), it is a good idea to do a rough sketch first. Then fill in the shaded part with letters and symbols.

If the typewriter has a ribbon that types red and black, you can use both colours to make your pictures more dramatic.

Don't forget to ask permission first if you are using a typewriter that is not your own.

Here are some examples of typewriter pictures. You need practice and lots of patience.

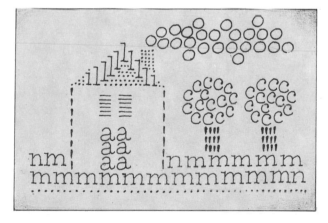

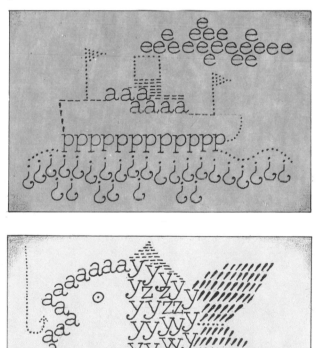

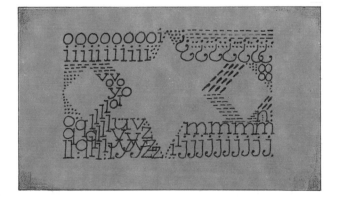

Camembert mastered all the more complicated parts of the office routine. He found it very satisfying to be able to write out telegrams, receipts and money orders, all with the correct number of copies. If you enjoy organization and paperwork too, why not set up an office at home.

An Office at Home

For a really professional look use a typewriter and make carbon copies of your notices for all your friends. But this is not absolutely necessary; small notebooks typed with each person's name can be used instead. Have fun setting up a club and issuing official-looking documents for it. Here are a few examples—not just to be copied, but to spark off some ideas of your own.

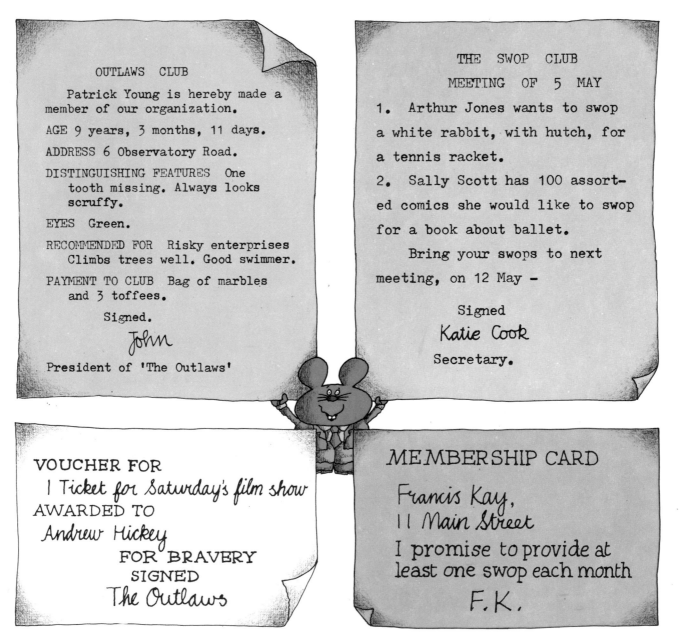

OUTLAWS CLUB

        Patrick Young is hereby made a member of our organization.

AGE 9 years, 3 months, 11 days.

ADDRESS 6 Observatory Road.

DISTINGUISHING FEATURES One tooth missing. Always looks scruffy.

EYES Green.

RECOMMENDED FOR Risky enterprises Climbs trees well. Good swimmer.

PAYMENT TO CLUB Bag of marbles and 3 toffees.

        Signed.

        John

President of 'The Outlaws'

THE SWOP CLUB
MEETING OF 5 MAY

1. Arthur Jones wants to swop a white rabbit, with hutch, for a tennis racket.

2. Sally Scott has 100 assorted comics she would like to swop for a book about ballet.

        Bring your swops to next meeting, on 12 May –

        Signed
        Katie Cook
        Secretary.

VOUCHER FOR
1 Ticket for Saturday's film show
AWARDED TO
Andrew Hickey
        FOR BRAVERY
        SIGNED
        The Outlaws

MEMBERSHIP CARD

Francis Kay,
11 Main Street
I promise to provide at least one swop each month
        F.K.

At the Post Office the work went on the same as usual. All the letters and parcels that people brought in had to be weighed, if necessary, and stamped. Then everything was put into the special boxes for collection.

Of course some times were busier than others. At Christmas Camembert would disappear under piles of mail for hours at a time and tea breaks became just pleasant memories. Reginald and Camembert organized all the bags for the mail that went by train.

The Mail Train Game

Every day thousands of letters and parcels are carried by train. But, although we take our morning post for granted, it wasn't always like this. Before the postal service began, if you wanted to send a message to a friend in another part of the country, you had to wait until someone you knew was travelling to that place.

But in 1840 Sir Rowland Hill invented the postage stamp, and, to make sure that stamped letters got to their destinations quickly, horses were organized to carry mail up and down the country. After that came mail coaches, and eventually mail trains.

Today, of course, mail is also sent by air and ship so that no part of the world is out of reach. Although very complex machinery is now used in the larger post offices—for sorting letters, for example —the post is still put through your letterbox by a postman, just as it was when the postal service started in the nineteenth century.

The Rules

A board for the Mail Train Game is printed on the next two pages. Any number of people can play. You need a dice and a button, coin or piece of card for each player to use as a counter.

Each player writes the messages he wishes to send on small pieces of paper. The papers are folded, so that no one can read what is written, and then thoroughly shuffled. You need 34 messages—one for each square on the board.

Put a message on each square. Throw the dice to see who starts—the first person to throw a six begins.

The first player moves his counter the same number of squares on the board as shown by the dice. Then he picks up the message on that square, reads it and does whatever it says!

Everyone throws the dice in turn. Throwing a six always gives you the chance of another throw, which can be useful if you don't like your first message!

The Mail Train Game

The Mail Train Game

When a counter passes square 34, it waits in the train's engine until its player throws two sixes in a row—then it goes back to the beginning again.

The game is over when all the messages have been picked up. Of course there is no winner—the object of the game is to have as much fun as possible. The more original and amusing the messages, the better the game.

Here are just a few suggestions for messages—but try to think up some funny ones of your own.

1. The mail train has been attacked by a dangerous gang. You must give the player on your right all that's in your left-hand pocket, and the player on your left all that's in your right-hand pocket.

2. You have landed on the sleeping car. For the rest of the game you must play lying down.

3. The engine is stoked up. Speed on three squares.

4. An enemy is chasing you. Disguise yourself so he won't recognize you on the journey.

5. You have been caught without a ticket. Subtract one from each of your next three throws of the dice.

6. The train has stopped at a red signal Miss two turns.

7. The whistle has broken. You must whistle all through the next round.

8. You are passing through some beautiful countryside. Before you move on you must name three yellow flowers.

9. You have been given a dog ticket by mistake. For the next three rounds you must play on all fours, bark and throw the dice with your teeth.

After a while Reginald suggested that Camembert should come and live with him. His house would be much more comfortable than the rather cramped mousehole where Camembert was living. So Camembert packed the few belongings he had and arrived on his friend's doorstep.

But if Reginald's life at the Post Office was boring, Camembert soon found that his life at home was, if possible, worse! Every day he followed a dull routine, doing the same thing at the same hour, so that there were never any surprises. Camembert almost wished there was a cat around for a little excitement.

In the mornings they had break-fast together and then did the house-work before going to work. On the way home from work they did the shopping. Reginald had got into the habit of always having two boiled eggs chopped up in a mug, for supper, because it was quick and easy.

'If you eat any more eggs,' said Camembert one evening, 'you'll grow feathers!' But Reginald didn't hear him, because he was engrossed in his stamp collection.

'I must do something to break this routine,' said Camembert to himself. 'If I don't watch out, I'll become fat and lazy like my Turkish uncle, and I don't have six beautiful pink-eyed wives to wait upon me! No, some-thing has got to be done.'

So the days went by at Reginald's house. Each one was exactly the same as the one before, like the sheep Camembert counted jumping over fences when he couldn't get to sleep. The little mouse now had a comfortable bed in Reginald's pipe.

How to make a Stamp Collection

To make a stamp collection, save all the used envelopes you can find. Ask your friends to look out for any foreign stamps for you and to send you post-cards if they are abroad on holiday. Sometimes stamps with special pictures are issued, so watch for those. There are usually colourful ones at Christmas time.

When you have collected a pile, soak the stamps off their backing—don't tear them off or you will ruin them. Put them in a bowl with some tepid water and a little salt to help them keep their colour.

After about twenty minutes, put them in a bowl of cold water and they will peel away quite easily from the bits of envelope.

When they are clean and separate, place them carefully between two sheets of blotting paper inside a book to dry flat.

A magnifying glass is useful for checking the details of your stamps. If you want to be really professional, you will need a perforation guide to measure the perforations along the sides of each stamp and a watermark checker.

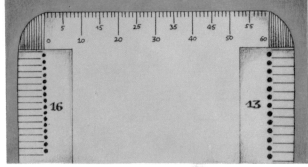

One thing you will need is a stamp album. But there is no need to buy one. You can make one easily by filling a ring-binder file with sheets of thick paper.

Never stick stamps straight on to the sheets of your album. Fix them on with stamp hinges. Then you will be able to pick them up to look at them closely, or move them around the pages of your album.

Arrange your stamps by countries or by themes. Fill a page with stamps showing pictures of birds, flowers, famous people, aeroplanes or buildings.

Always fix your stamps in the album so that you look at the oldest issues first and the newest ones last.

Just for Fun

Perhaps you think making your own stamp collection seems like an awful lot of hard work? Well, there is a much easier way of collecting stamps, although the result will be worth nothing—except a few laughs.

Think up ideas for special stamps, draw them on paper, colour them in and cut them out. Give them crinkly edges like the perforations you find on real stamps. If you want to try and fool people, fix them in among some real stamps in an album.

Of course, you can't use home-made stamps for sending letters through the post. The Post Office just wouldn't think it was funny!

You can make a cancelling stamp from a cork. Draw a design, or your initial (in reverse) on the end. Carefully cut away the cork from round the design. Now you can use the stamp, with an inkpad or some thick paint, to cancel your stamped letters, the way they do in the Post Office.

Mr Gorgonzola,
Camembert House,
Timbuctu,
AFRICA.

While his friend snored gently, Camembert would think aloud to himself:

'Whatever can I do to make something happen? If this goes on much longer, I'll become ill from boredom. If only, I were rich, like my Arab uncle, Sheik Atail, I could take Reginald on a trip round the world. Then he would see for himself that there's more to life than a cup of cocoa at the end of the day!'

Although Camembert was becoming more and more cheesed off with life at Reginald's, he felt he couldn't just abandon his friend. After all, a friend in need is a friend indeed. And Camembert was beginning to feel that Reginald was in need—of a small bomb under him!

The alarm clock rang each morning at seven o'clock sharp. Reginald had a hot shower while Camembert made the breakfast. Breakfast was

always the same, of course—coffee and toast. Even tea and cornflakes would have been a change. While Reginald got dressed, he always listened to *The Flight of the Bumble Bee*, which was his favourite piece of music. Camembert thought he would go mad if he heard that tune once more.

'Perhaps I could marry off Reginald to Miss Cooper of Air Mail,' he wondered. 'Then I would be free to go off by myself.' But it looked as if Reginald was a confirmed bachelor.

Chapter Two
SUNDAY MORNING

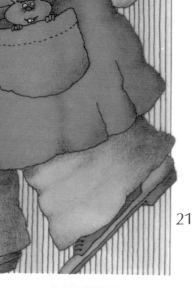

The only days when Reginald's routine varied were Sundays and holidays. Then, instead of getting up at seven o'clock, they got up at eight. Instead of having toast for breakfast, they had hot rolls. And of course they didn't go to the Post Office. In the morning they went down to the Old Market to find some stamps for Reginald's collection. After lunch, instead of doing something different like going to a football match or the seaside, Reginald went off to his stamp-collecting club, where they all swopped stamps and boasted about their collections.

But one Sunday something different happened.

It began like any other Sunday. Camembert was warm and snug in the pocket of Reginald's raincoat, as usual. They took the bus to the Old Market, as they did every Sunday.

Camembert was quite resigned to the same old routine when, believe it or not, something very unusual happened.

Instead of going straight towards the stamp stalls, as he usually did, Reginald stopped to look in a shop window. It was a junk shop, full of all kinds of strange things, from a four-poster bed to a suit of armour.

The shop owner appeared at the window with a metal lamp in his hands.

'Here's a fine object,' he said. 'It belonged to an Eastern king who lost all his money at the races.'

But what would Reginald want a lamp for? In any case it was all dirty and dented.

The shop owner was so insistent that the lamp was a bargain, that Reginald was forced to ask the price.

'How much is it?'

'The price is marked here.'

'Sorry—that's much too dear.'

'All right, how much would you pay?'

'Five—and that's my limit.'
'Say six and it's a deal!'
And so the bargaining went on.

The Bargaining Game

So the shop owner and Reginald bargained back and forth. Driving a bargain really means finding a solution to a conflict. Of course, all sorts of conflict crop up in life—and also in play and stories.

Perhaps you know the famous story of Romeo and Juliet. They are in love, but their families hate each other and try to keep them apart.

There are many stories in which the excitement comes from conflict. The hero wants one thing and the 'villain' another. Some well-known examples are Robin Hood and the Sheriff of Nottingham, Sherlock Holmes and the evil Moriarti—even Little Red Riding Hood and the wolf?

The stories would be very boring if there was no conflict in them. If Little Red Riding Hood set out to visit her grandmother, had a pleasant tea and went home again, who would be interested enough to read to the end of the story?

Bargaining is a very simple and clear-cut form of conflict. One person wants to buy something at the cheapest possible price, and the other wants to sell it at the highest possible price.

Imagine it is a very hot day, and a boy is strolling along a beach with a water melon under his arm. Another boy rushes up to him and begs him to sell it to him, as he is dying of thirst.

'All right,' says the boy, 'but it will cost you so much.'

'But I've only got half that amount!'

'I couldn't possibly sell this fine juicy melon for as little as that.'

And so it goes on.

You can bargain for almost anything. And it needn't just be between two people. In an auction, lots of people are involved.

'What am I bid?' asks the auctioneer, and everyone calls out their bids until only one person is left—the person willing to pay the highest price for the article.

Use Your Imagination

The junk shop Reginald visited was overflowing with old, unusual objects. If you enjoy acting, why not pretend to be an object that appeals to you?

Can you guess what the three children in the picture below are?

Of course it is much harder acting

An old chair complained about the dampness. A bright young kettle twinkled and suggested they should hold a party. A violin played a sad little tune to itself.

It is easy to think up lots of other things which are not in the picture, and

the part of a clock or a dustbin, than a princess or a wizard. But there is more scope for your imagination.

Reginald and Camembert at last left the shop with the old lamp. The shop owner put the money in the till, pulled the blinds, turned out the lights and went off home.

Then, in the darkness, the objects in the shop yawned, stretched and began to talk to each other!

Some of the objects said what bad luck it was that their old friend the lamp had been sold. He had gone away into the wide world—who knew what would happen to him? Would his new owner look after and polish him—or would he neglect him?

to give them their own personalities.

A doll with a china face and fine clothes who is used to much better things. A whistle with a cold. A table which limps about with one leg shorter than the others. A sword that has been to many famous battles and is always boasting about his bravery.

If you and your friends pretend to be different objects, and all speak to each other about your experiences, you have an instant play!

The shop owner had persuaded Reginald after a lot of haggling, to buy the old dirty battered lamp. And for quite a high price, too!

'Why on earth did you let him talk you into it?' asked Camembert.

'I don't really know. I felt sorry for him, I suppose. Perhaps he needs the money.'

'He needs the money? What I was a bit of an idiot, wasn't I?'

But one person was quite happy— the shop owner, who had sold the lamp for five times the price he had paid for it himself!

Reginald spent all of the rest of that day complaining about his bad luck.

'Everyone takes advantage of my good nature. Why did I let myself be

about us? How much have you got left?'

Reginald looked in his wallet, then felt in each of his pockets.

'Nothing. I've spent it all.'

'So how are you going to buy your stamps?'

'We'll just have to go back home.

talked into such a thing? Not only do I not need a lamp, this one is old and broken. When I think of what I could have spent that money on— a matching tie and handkerchief for the office, or a new alarm clock that wakes you with flashing lights and a cup of tea!'

Of course, he was quite right, the lamp looked even worse out of the junk shop. And a bit of the handle was missing.

Reginald suddenly stood up and shouted, 'I'm going to throw it in the dustbin. I'm sick of the sight of it!'

Camembert tried to stop him.

'There's no point in throwing it away now! All right—you bought it on impulse. That's not in your nature, but you must learn to make the best of things. We could use it as a sauce boat, or a paperweight, or a bathtub for me!'

'But it's so dirty, Camembert. It's covered with grime.'

'Well we can clean it, can't we? One of my distant cousins, Pat O'Flannel, is an Irish tinker and he taught me everything there is to know about cleaning and polishing.'

Camembert was just about to start rubbing the lamp with a soft cloth, when a strange thought went through his head. The lamp re-minded him of an old Eastern tale about a magic lamp with a genie inside it. As soon as you rubbed the lamp, the genie came out. He was so grateful to be free at last, that he granted the owner of the lamp three wishes.

'Don't be silly, Camembert,' said Reginald. 'There's no need to be frightened, genies don't exist.'

'You think so, do you?' asked Camembert. 'You think that all the tales about them are just stupid stories? Well, I'm not sure. I've travelled a great deal and I've seen many strange and wonderful things. And this lamp is so old, it's just the sort of lamp a genie would live in. Just think if there is one—he will open up a whole new world for us!'

Camembert gave Reginald the duster. 'Come on, have a go. What harm can it do?'

So Reginald began to rub half-heartedly, grumbling all the time. Nothing happened.

'What did I tell . . .' he began, when he suddenly stopped, and looked at Camembert in amazement. A loud yawn had come out of the lamp's spout!

'Listen!' cried Camembert. 'It's a

genie! He's probably been asleep for thousands of years, and will need a lot of rubbing to wake him up.'

He grabbed the duster from Reginald, and began to rub hard with both hands.

'Don't stop now,' said Reginald, beginning to get excited at last.

Soon a thin column of smoke snaked its way out of the lamp's spout. Reginald's eyes grew larger.

Camembert rubbed and rubbed until, bit by bit, the column of smoke grew into a huge cloud, with arms, a face and a rather fierce-looking moustache!

Even Reginald couldn't mistake what it was. It was a genie!

Well, Camembert had longed for something to happen and now it had! Even he, who took a pride in never being surprised at anything, was taken aback.

As for Reginald—he was beginning to wish he'd gone to his stamp-collectors club after all!

But there was no going back now. It seemed amazing that such a huge genie had come out of so tiny a lamp. And they couldn't possibly squash him back in, even if they had wanted to.

As the genie floated gently against the familiar background of his sitting-room, Reginald knew his dull life would never be the same again. At the back of his mind, however, his old self was saying, 'I hope the neighbours don't see it. Whatever would they think?'

Guide to Stain Removal

It's unlikely you have many old lamps to clean, but nearly everyone comes across an ink stain at some time. Mop up as soon as possible with blotting paper or newspaper, then sponge with hot soapy water.

Rust marks can be quite tough to remove. Try covering the stains with salt and then squeezing lemon juice on top. Wash immediately afterwards, or the lemon juice will take the colour out of the fabric.

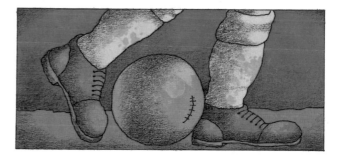

Try to clean up blood stains before they have had time to dry. Soak in cold water, with some salt added, for a couple of hours. The stains should then wash out easily.

Let mud dry on a garment before brushing it off with a hard brush. Then wash with soapy water with a little vinegar added. Rinse well in plenty of cold water.

Wax stains are usually stubborn. Scrape off as much as possible with a knife. Then ask your mother, next time she's ironing, to press the fabric between two sheets of blotting paper (or old towels). A little methylated spirits will remove any mark that's left.

You're bound to come across a tea, chocolate or coffee stain at some time. Soak the garment in cold water, then wash in the usual way. On a carpet, wipe with plenty of cold water, to dilute the stain, leave to dry and use a dry cleaning fluid if necessary.

Chapter Three

THE GENIE OF THE LAMP

The genie seemed to be quite wide awake now. He was very glad to have someone to talk to, after his years alone, and he told Reginald and Camembert all about his past.

He had lived for a long time in the desert, where he worked as assistant to a lamp-maker. It was not very interesting work, so he passed a lot of the time in playing practical jokes.

He buried travellers' food supplies in the sand; he tied tins to camels' tails; he imitated the howls of wild animals outside peoples' tents late at night. You can imagine how popular he was!

Make a Floating Genie

It's easy to make a floating genie. Blow up the biggest balloon you can find. Cut out shapes for the eyes, nose and mouth, as shown. Cut the hair, moustache, eyebrows and beard out of tissue paper, so that they float well. Glue in position.

Ask your father to suspend your genie from the ceiling with sticky tape. It will move in any draughts.

Here are some more balloon heads for you to copy.

Papier Mâché Puppet

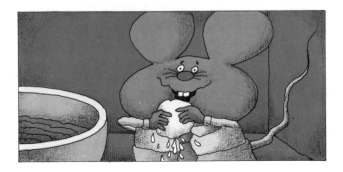

You can also use a balloon as the base to make a papier mâché puppet. To make the papier mâché, tear old newspapers into small pieces. Put them into a bowl half-filled with cold water and add

a little glue (the kind used for gluing models). The mixture should be fairly stiff. Knead it until it begins to stick to your fingers. It's ready when it's good and sticky.

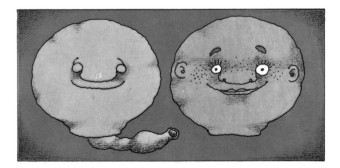

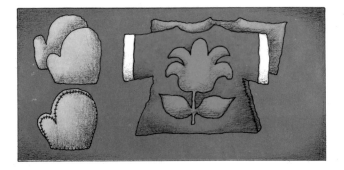

To make the head, blow-up a balloon to the right size. Cover with the papier mâché and leave to dry thoroughly—overnight, at least. Then let the air out and pull the balloon out gently. Paint on a face.

Cut hands out of pale felt and the body out of brightly-coloured fabric. Cut out of a double thickness of fabric for two of everything. Sew or glue together, on the wrong side, and join hands to body.

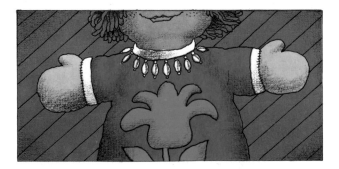

Now glue or tape the body to the head.

Disguise the join with a necklace made of beads or a scarf

Arrange your fingers and thumb inside the puppet, as shown, and practise moving the head and arms by wiggling your fingers.

One day a wizard came to the village and asked him the way to the nearest oasis. The genie, who was feeling rather bored at the time, sent him off in the opposite direction. The wizard, after hours of wandering, bumped into a tribe of fierce people who hated strangers. By the time he arrived back at the genie's village, he was covered in bruises and scratches, and was very angry indeed.

So in revenge he cast a spell over the lamp-maker's assistant, turning him into a genie imprisoned in one of his master's lamps. And there he had stayed, ending up in all sorts of places with other junk, until today.

'And now,' he finished, 'I am at your command.'

'I know,' said Camembert, 'I've read about you in books. Although I never dreamed I would meet a genie in the flesh. Or whatever it is,' he added thoughtfully.

Camembert had fetched his book about genies. It was just as he had thought. Anyone who helped a genie escape from his prison, was

33

entitled to three wishes, which the genie would grant.

But what would they ask for? Wealth or happiness? To become invisible? To be witty and handsome so that everyone would like them? They could become the most important people in the Post Office, or they could choose never to work again. They could wish for never a dull moment for the rest of their lives.

'Let's take our time,' said Camembert. 'There's no point in asking for the first things that come into our heads. Once we've chosen our wishes, we can never have another chance.'

Reginald was looking stunned by the whole experience. Camembert saw that he would need time to recover. And he would need time to think. But what about the genie? It did seem cruel to leave him hanging around, waiting, after all those years asleep. What could he suggest to keep him amused for a while?

'I know,' said Camembert, 'I'll show you the Monsters game.'

The Monsters Game

Any number can play. Each person has a thin piece of cardboard, all the same colour, and all divided into nine equal squares numbered 1–9, on the back. Everyone draws a monster—the more horrible the better—on the front of his card.

Now the squares are cut up and mixed together. Shuffle well and deal out, face down.

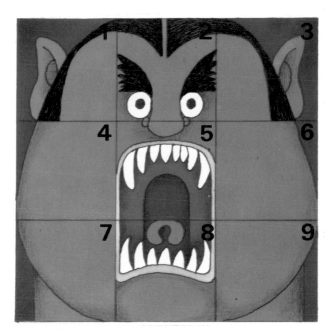

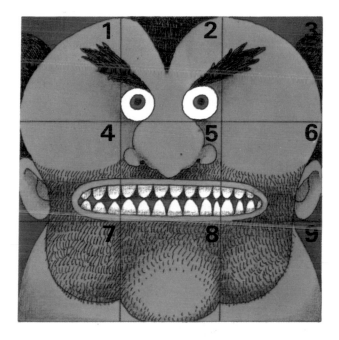

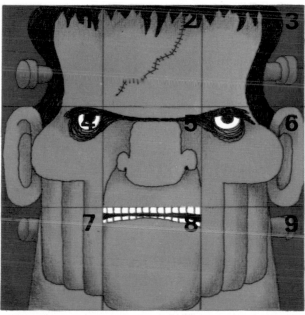

The first player must play a card numbered 1. The second player plays a number 2, next to the number 1. If he doesn't have a 2, he can start a new monster with another number 1. If he has neither of these, he must pass.

The game continues like this, and the winner is the one who gets rid of all his cards first.

As you can see, all the parts of each monster's head will fit into the others. In this way, you can produce even more revolting monsters!

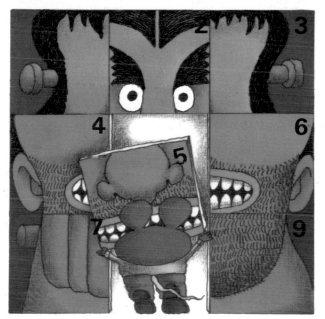

Suddenly Reginald had an idea. 'I know!, I'd like one of the special 1851 issue of Hawaii stamps!'

The genie wasn't very pleased. That didn't give him much scope to use his magic powers! 'But Master, anyone could have that without the help of a genie. That's not a great wish.'

'Oh but it is,' said Reginald. 'You see, those stamps are extremely rare and very valuable. I've got a special page in my stamp album, just waiting for one.'

'I don't care. You should ask me for something magic, something difficult, something worthy of a genie!'

Camembert was hopping up and down. He was dying for some excitement, and here was Reginald about to throw away a wish on a stamp!

'Could you suggest something?' he asked the genie.

The genie puffed out his chest. 'I could take you on a wonderful journey, through time and space. You would travel in comfort, without any effort on your part, and we would visit only the most splendid sights. Would you like that?'

'Oh yes,' squeaked Camembert.

Chapter Four
IN THE DESERT

One moment Reginald and Camembert were in Reginald's sitting-room. The next they were surrounded by scorched sand, as far as their eyes could see. It must be a desert!

'Is this what you call a wonderful place?' asked Camembert in disgust.

'Well, I like it—I was born here,' said the genie.

'Oh, this is dreadful,' said Reginald. 'I thought we would end up somewhere *interesting*, like the Eiffel Tower or the Statue of Liberty. What can the genie be thinking of?'

The hot sun beating down made both of them realize that they were not at all equipped for spending any time in a desert. They had neither food nor water, and there were lots of other things they would need.

'Would you like to go home now?' asked the genie, with a smug expression which irritated Camembert.

Reginald opened his mouth to say

'Yes', but Camembert stopped him in time.

'Certainly not,' he said. 'We can get out of this by ourselves—without any help from anyone with magic powers.'

Camembert was feeling more and more sorry for Reginald, who looked as if he was about to faint from the heat at any moment. He was not used to long treks either. The longest distance he usually walked was to the bus stop!

Camembert, however, felt at home anywhere. He had already visited the desert on one of his adventures, and led the way in the direction in which he thought they would find an oasis.

All the time the sun beat down on them.

The genie floated along beside them, suggesting from time to time, 'Would you like me to produce a cool sea breeze or a shower of rain?' When no one answered, he went on, 'How about a fountain of iced water, just here?'

But Camembert ignored him. He was sure they could fall back on their own resources. 'We must protect our heads from the sun's rays. There's always a danger of sunstroke here. We also need fans and water bottles.'

Desert Equipment

How to make a Sun Hat

You need a piece of card, a handkerchief, glue and string. Cut out the shape shown by the dotted line, make two holes for the string and attach the handkerchief, as shown. This will protect your eyes and the nape of your neck.

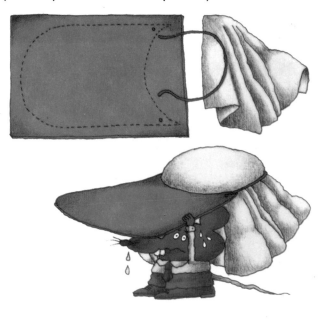

How to make a Fan

Make the fan from a piece of card or balsa wood.

Draw on the outline of the shape you want—a simple circle, or something more imaginative like one of the other shapes shown here. Cut out with scissors, or with a special small saw if you are using balsa wood.

The handle is a small stick or length of wood.

Cut a notch in the top to fit the fan into and strengthen by winding string tightly round it.

When your fan is finished paint it, or glue on pictures cut out of old magazines to make a collage.

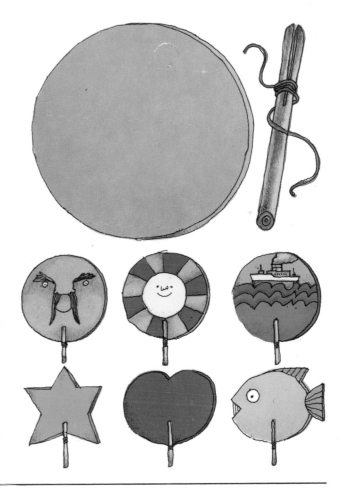

How to make a Water Bottle

You need a flattish bottle for this. Make the cover from canvas or thick flannel. Place the bottle on the material, and draw round it—twice, as shown. Leave a good margin all round, and position buttons and buttonholes as shown. Or fasten with sewn-on poppers. If the cover is wet thoroughly and left in the open air, it will keep any liquid cool for a long time.

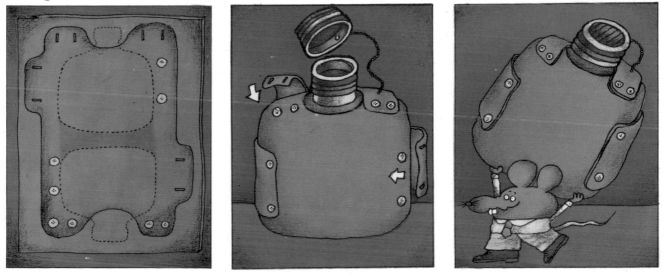

A CARAVAN!

As the day wore on, it began to get a bit cooler. Suddenly Reginald and Camembert saw some men on camels coming up to their oasis.

Luckily for them, the caravan wasn't made up of bandits or robbers, but of traders who went from oasis to oasis, selling their wares. They could travel for days without coming across anyone, so they were delighted to see some new faces. Soon everyone was talking and telling each other stories.

Reginald told them what had happened to them, with long pauses for heaving sighs and wiping of glasses. The traders stared at him—they had never come across anyone like him before.

But when he came to the bit about the genie, they all laughed heartily and slapped their knees. They had all heard old stories about the genie who played practical jokes.

'Ho! Ho!' they guffawed, 'Really, it's enough to make a camel laugh! But you mustn't think we're all like that.'

40

They invited Reginald to a desert supper of dates, dried figs and nuts.

It looked as if the genie was sulking. He wasn't used to being ignored. As there was much less to him than met the eye—he was just a mass of air with no stomach or anything—he wasn't interested in food. But that didn't stop him saying, when the food arrived, 'I could have prepared a wonderful supper—much better than this snack!'

Camembert glared at him. Reginald said to the traders, 'What a magnificent spread! Can you give me some of your recipes?'

Supper in the Desert

Dried figs, dates and nuts are the fruits of the desert. Use them to make some sweets to enjoy with your friends, or to

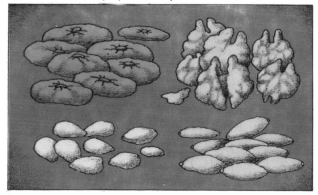

put in a pretty box and give as a present.

Take the tops and tails off some dried figs, press a small nut inside and add a drop of honey.

Dates make lovely sweets. Stone them, halve them and fill the centres with marzipan.

When the sweets are all ready, put them into paper cases and sprinkle with a little castor sugar.

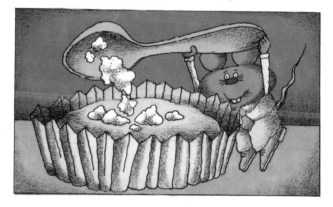

After their supper, they all sat round and talked. The traders told them stories about their wanderings in the desert.

Now that the sun was going down, it was growing quite cold.

'Why don't we play a game before it gets dark?' suggested someone. 'Something energetic, to warm us all up.'

'What about that new game they're playing in Mecca? What's it called? Oh yes, the Four Oases Game!'

The Four Oases Game

This is a game played by desert nomads when they have set up camp and have some time on their hands.

You can play it too. It needs eleven

their backs to become riders.

When the Chief blows his whistle again, everyone has to change his oasis for another one. After a reasonable

players, so it's a good game for the school playground.

Mark out four oases on the ground, as shown. Five players will be camels, and five others riders mounted on the camels' backs. The eleventh player is the chief of the tribe and starts the game off. If you have a dice, take turns in throwing it. The first person to throw a six is the Chief. You also need a whistle. To start the game, the Chief blows the whistle. At once each camel and its rider tries to occupy one of the four oases.

One of the five will, of course, be unlucky, and that camel, with its rider, is out of the game.

The Chief blows his whistle again. The four riders left, get down to have a drink at the oasis. The camels' then get on

length of time, he blows his whistle. Any camel with its rider who has failed to get into an oasis is out of the game. Part of the game is to try and stop other camels from getting to an oasis.

Once safely installed in an oasis, no one can attack a camel and rider, except when they're changing roles. The pair who were put out of the game at first, can try their luck at getting into it again.

To find a new Chief, stop the game and have a camel race.

Camel races are like horse races—so you play them on all fours. But as camels have humps on their backs, each person must carry two objects on his back. These can be boxes, baskets, books—even flowerpots (plastic ones).

A camel who drops a 'hump' is

disqualified. To make it easier, have a dromedary race. Dromedaries only have one hump!

After the camel race, have a rider's race. The riders must race with their tongues hanging out, as if they have been riding through the desert dust and and are very thirsty. Anyone who forgets, and closes his mouth is disqualified!

You should now have two winners—

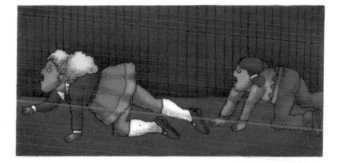

one from the camels and one from the riders.

The Chief's whistle is put down on the desert sand (the ground) and the two winners must try to find it blindfolded. The finder is the new Chief.

The new Chief chooses five new camels and five riders. The game continues until everyone is tired out or, if you're playing at school, the bell rings!

Camembert and Reginald were tired but happy after their supper and games.

The traders had promised to take them to an airport only two days' travel away, in the morning. So soon they would be flying home!

The genie was still sulking. Reginald seemed to have no wish for him to carry out. He looked over, grumpily, to where the nomad chief was reciting his favourite poem.

'And the night shall be filled with
  music,
And the cares that infest the day,
Shall fold their tents like the Arabs,
And silently, steal away.'

'Hmph! Very apt!' said the genie.
'Just you wait.'

Night fell, and the nomad traders
lit a fire, because it gets very cold in
the desert at night.

Everyone sat round the flames.
The genie was becoming even more
fed up.

He had been elbowed out, away
from the fire, and forced to sit at the
back beside the camels. He was not
used to such treatment. He had
thought that, having escaped from
his prison, he would be greeted
everywhere with awe and amazement.

The nomads told Camembert
what a hard life they led. 'We have
no modern luxuries. Our dream is to
have a record player, so we can play
our copy of "The Desert Song".'

Nomad Orchestra

You can make the stringed instruments
shown here. They are similar to the ones
used by the nomad traders in the
desert. They made them out of old tins
and pots, after they had eaten their
supplies out of them. The instruments
are made out of old biscuit tins of
different shapes, without lids. You also
need some guitar strings, of different
thicknesses so that they produce

different sounds when plucked or strummed.

A very strange instrument can be made out of a funnel with a length of rubber pipe fitted into it. It will make a very unusual noise when blown—deep and loud, and quite unlike any other musical instrument.

If you can find an earthenware pot and a piece of thin leather, you can make another original instrument.

Soak the leather in water overnight. Then stretch it over the neck of the pot and tie it down tightly, as shown. As the leather dries out, it will become tightly stretched. Now the lightest touch on the taut surface will produce a sound, and it has become an excellent drum.

If you want an instrument which will give you every note in the scale, fill a row of bottles with water to different levels.

Adjust the level of the water in each bottle, until you get the note you want when it is struck. Ask a friend with a good musical ear to help you tune your instrument.

If all the bottles are the same size and type (for example, milk bottles) it will make the tuning easier.

Now you have your instruments, all you need is a tune. Practise with friends. If you can read music, you can follow a tune on your bottle instrument. The drum and funnel are a little more crude, but they can still be used to great effect.

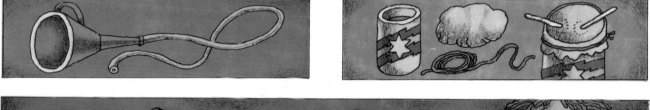

In the meantime, the traders had to make their own music. They decided to give a concert that very evening, in honour of their visitors, using strange old instruments that they had made themselves.

Before putting out the fire and going off to their tents, the nomads asked Reginald for something to remember him by.

Camembert said this wasn't necessary, as they would all be travelling together for a couple of days yet. But the traders said it would be better to get it over with now. And every day they asked for something else. Even Reginald's watch found its way into one of the deep pockets in their robes.

When Reginald and Camembert were alone, they agreed that they were worried, 'I wonder if these gentlemen are as nice as they seemed to be at first?' said Reginald.

The genie came up to them and said, 'If my Masters wish it, I can tell them what kind of people these are.'

'Thank you, but when we want something, we'll let you know,' said Camembert firmly.

45

'All right,' said the genie, 'I'll tell you anyway. They are the famous desert robbers, the descendants of Ali Baba!'

But Reginald and Camembert didn't seem interested. They were dreaming about home comforts. How they missed a warm, soothing nightcap—or a cool refreshing drink in the heat of the day.

'When I get home,' sighed Reginald, 'the first thing I'm going to do is go straight to the kitchen. I wonder if I can still remember my recipes?'

While Camembert and Reginald slept at last, the genie lay awake all night, trying to think up a plan.

At last, when it was almost dawn, he remembered a spell for making people vanish.

Reginald's Recipes

Here are a few recipes from the Drinks section of Reginald's recipe book:

Green Oasis

(Serves 4)

Ingredients:
¾ litre (1½ pints) diluted lime cordial
syrup from 1 medium can of pear halves
juice of 1 lemon
ice cubes
4 lemon slices

What to do:
Mix lime juice with pear syrup and lemon juice. Pour into 4 glasses, and put 2 ice cubes in each. Slit each lemon slice from centre to outside edge and place on rim of glasses. Serve!

Tailnote

If you make Green Oasis, you will be left with a few pear halves, drained of their syrup. Camembert suggests you make these into his favourite party dish, Cheesy Mice.

Minted Hot Chocolate

(Serves 3)

Ingredients:
3 rounded teaspoons drinking chocolate
4 peppermint cream sweets, crumbled
½ litre (1 pint) milk
3 small chocolate flake bars

What to do:
Put drinking chocolate, peppermint creams and milk together in a saucepan. Heat milk very slowly to boiling point stirring from time to time until the sweets have dissolved. Pour into a bowl and whisk well. Pour drink into 3 mugs and pop a flake bar into each instead of a spoon.

Cheesy Mice

Ingredients:
pear halves (1 for each person)
1 small packet cream cheese
a little French dressing or mayonnaise
crisp lettuce leaves
few black grapes
few split, blanched almonds
few currants
pieces of string

What to do:
In a bowl, blend the cream cheese with a little dressing or mayonnaise, stirring well until the mixture is soft and will spread easily. Using a knife, spread the cream cheese mixture all over the rounded side of each pear half. Place each pear half on a plate on top of a lettuce leaf. Put half a black grape on each side of the sharper end, for eyes. Two split, blanched almonds make ears. A currant is the nose. Lastly, stick a piece of clean string into the other end for a tail!

Desert Cooler

(Serves 2)

Ingredients:
1 small carton raspberry flavour yogurt
1 glass fizzy lemonade
2 tablespoons vanilla ice cream

What to do:
Whisk the yogurt and lemonade together quickly in a bowl. Place a spoonful of ice cream in each glass. Pour on the yogurt and lemonade and serve at once.

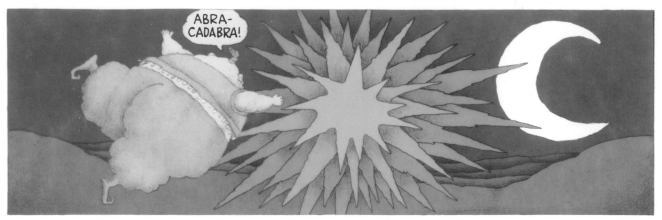

Reginald and Camembert woke to hear the genie saying 'Wake up! Wake up! You need no longer fear the evil robbers I have made them vanish with a magic spell!'

'But now we're even worse off than we were before!' said Camembert.

'I thought I was helping,' said the genie. 'After all, they were robbers, but I could make them reappear.'

'Don't do anything else,' said Camembert quickly.

How to make a Sand Timer

You need two small bottles with very thin necks, some glue or sticky tape and some fine sand. Fill one of the bottles with sand, using a piece of paper rolled into a cone to make a funnel, as shown. The other bottle should be placed neck down, balancing on top of the sand-filled bottle.

Before you stick the two bottles together, measure the amount of time the sand takes to run from one bottle into the other.

If the sand runs through too fast, not giving you enough time to boil an egg, for example, the necks of the bottles

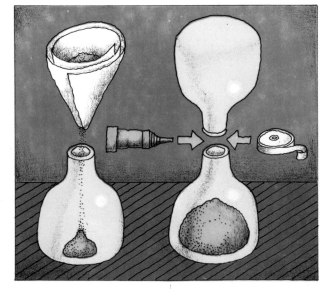

are too big. Get hold of a small washer, and insert this between the two bottles. The sand will then run more slowly through the hole in the washer.

To make the timer more stable, make small platforms for the top and bottom, joined together by canes or small sticks of wood.

Paint the wood brightly or finish off with a coat of clear varnish.

Many years ago, before people had clocks or wrist watches they had to rely on sand timers and, less commonly, water clocks. The other means of telling the time was the sundial.

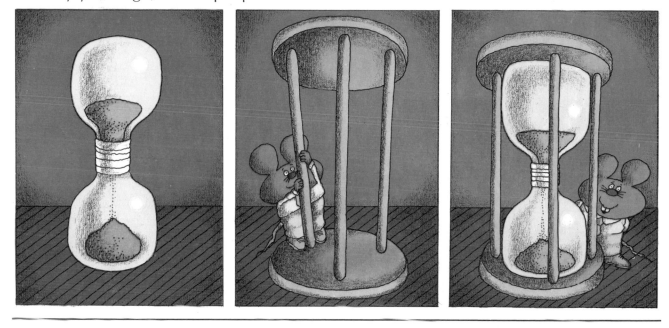

How to make a Sundial

Sundials were the clocks most often used long ago, because they didn't need water, sand or bottles. In fact, they needed only a simple rod.

To be really accurate a sundial should be marked out using precise mathematical and astronomical knowledge. But it is simple to make a sundial which tells you what 'o'clock' it is, without too much detail about the minutes.

At exactly midday stand facing the sun and stick a rod into the ground. Note the shadow it casts and write the figure 12 at the end of the shadow.

The next day get up at the crack of dawn and mark the spot where the end of your shadow falls, precisely at each hour. And there's your sundial!

If you can't face getting up at dawn,

mark the first hour when you are up. After all, if you're never up before a certain time, you don't need to know the time before then, do you?

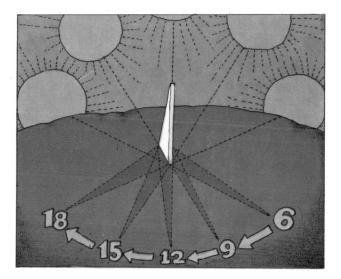

The genie couldn't stand waiting around doing nothing. He was beginning to feel rebellious. What was the use in having Masters who never wanted anything done?

He gave Reginald and Camembert a map. 'Maybe this will help you,' he said with a sly smile.

IF WE KNEW WHERE WE ARE

THIS MAP'S NO USE–IT'S FULL OF MISTAKES.

'Just what we need,' said Reginald, who, because of all his stamp-collecting, was an expert on geography and map-reading.

But when they looked closely at the map, their hopes fell again. It was a nonsense—everything was in the wrong place.

'It's to show you how stubborn you're being,' said the genie. 'You'll never get out of this on your own. I could conjure up a jeep with a tank full of petrol, and a hamper with cold chicken and chilled drinks in the back.'

But Camembert insisted that they would get out of the sticky situation by themselves. 'Every mouse likes a challenge,' he said.

Then the genie teased Reginald, asking him if he was a man or a mouse! Reginald was feeling upset by the heat anyway, and this was the last straw. He used up the second wish in wishing that the genie would be quiet!

So now they only had one wish left.

'Why don't we ask him to take us home?' asked Reginald.

'Rubbish,' said Camembert. 'I'm going off to get help. Promise me you won't use up the third wish while I'm gone.'

'All right, I promise.'

They agreed that Reginald and the genie would wait for four days for Camembert's return. If, after that time, he had still not come back, Reginald could have his third and last wish.

Chapter Five
HOMEWARD BOUND

Left alone with the genie, Reginald began to feel very guilty. He had stood back and let Camembert, who was, after all, only a small mouse, go off to look for help in the vast desert.

He, however, was all right. The nomad traders had left one of their tents behind. And, as a last resort, there was the genie. Reginald could never forget him—his huge shape always hovered in the background, although, unfortunately, it didn't seem to cast any shadow.

Feeling that he must do something, Reginald decided to pitch the tent and make a splendid camp, ready for Camembert's return. The genie watched his every move, waiting for a chance to distract him and make him waste his last wish. Then he would be free to go off on his own and get up to his old tricks.

'Thank goodness I was in the Scouts,' said Reginald to himself. 'It seems like only yesterday I was pitching tents and setting up camp with the Peewit Patrol.'

When Reginald had pitched his tent, he sat down and looked round him. But it was a depressing sight—the desert was completely barren.

How nice it would be if he could grow some plants and flowers round the tent, to welcome Camembert back.

But to grow plants he needed water and there was only one small spring at the oasis. 'I need seeds too,' said Reginald, 'and I'm sure Camembert wouldn't be very pleased if I used up the third wish on a packet of mixed annuals!'

Plants with a Difference

Plants can't live without water, but some can live with very little. Cactii, for example, are very easy to grow as house plants and need hardly any watering. That's why they grow so well in the desert.

There are many different kinds of cactus—some with beautiful flowers.

For a change, try growing plants by putting the seeds in water and feeding them with drops of plant food. If you put a layer of sand at the bottom, it will give the plants a base, as well as stopping the sun damaging their roots. Plants grow more quickly in water than in soil.

Of course, there was plenty of sunshine, which plants like. 'But I need sunshine, earth and water,' sighed Reginald, thinking fondly of his windowbox at home. He didn't know that you can grow plants with hardly any water, or with no earth at all.

Reginald was feeling more and more depressed. In this state of mind he was a very depressing person to have around. So the genie thought he had better try to cheer him up.

'Knock! knock!' he said.

'Who's there?' asked Reginald half-heartedly.

'Genie.'

'Genie who?' he couldn't stop himself asking.

'Genie with the light brown hair!'

Reginald just stared at him in disgust.

The genie tried again. 'What do you call an Arab dairy-farmer?'

'I don't know.'

'A milk Sheik!'

Still no response. 'Here's one that will really suit you if you sit out in this sun much longer—How can you tell that coconut juice is nutty?'

Without waiting for Reginald to answer the genie said triumphantly, 'Because it lives in a padded cell!'

Reginald still looked very un-amused.

Perhaps he had left his sense of humour at home! But the genie kept on chatting, as much to himself as to Reginald. 'The wizard who changed me into a genie was a great one for jokes. But of course some of them back-fired—like me! And that re-minds me, do you know why wizards drink lots of tea? Because sorcerers need cuppas!'

Reginald was feeling homesick

now. Where was Camembert and what was he doing? He began to think of all the things he would do when he got home.

There would be no more hot showers in the mornings for him. Oh no—they would be cold invigorating ones! And he would eat large, cool melons and chilled strawberries with ice cream. He could almost taste them! 'I never really thought about food before,' he said in surprise.

'Are you hungry?' asked the genie.

'What about a nice camel steak—one hump or two?'

Reginald decided that the best way to escape from the genie and his awful jokes was to go for a walk. He wandered off over the sand dunes and on his way he noticed quite a few stones of all shapes and sizes. These gave him an idea. He could grow nothing in the four days before Camembert's return, but he could decorate all the sand dunes round the oasis.

He set to work, and after a couple

of days the sand dunes looked amazing. Although the genie, of course, was not impressed.

'Why don't you let me cover the sand with roses, buttercups and daisies or huge sunflowers?' he asked.

'I've told you before, I don't want any help,' said Reginald.

'Is it your wish that I leave you alone?' asked the genie quickly, trying to trap Reginald.

'You know perfectly well what I mean, and it is not my third wish!' said Reginald. 'If only I had some paper, I could make some lovely paper flowers.'

How to make Paper Flowers

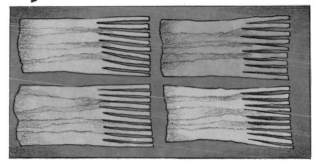

To make these flowers you need tissue or crepe paper, scissors and glue. Choose brightly coloured paper for the flower petals and green for the stem and calyx.

Cut the paper into rectangles of the length you want your flowers to be. Each flower is made up of two pieces of paper the same size—one for the outside and one for the inside.

Cut to almost halfway up the coloured paper, as shown, like a fringe. Twist the uncut part round to make a stem.

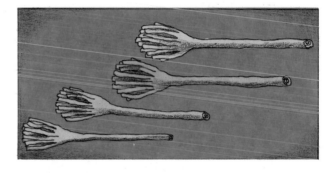

Now fringe the end of the green paper and spread a little glue over the uncut part. Wrap this tightly round the coloured stem, as shown, to make the finished flower.

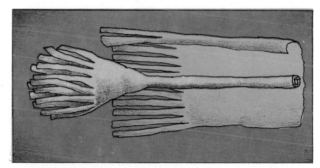

Leave the flowers to dry with their stems under a weight, like a heavy book. As well as stopping them unwinding, this will help make the stems rigid so that they stand up well in a vase.

Don't be impatient and put flowers in a vase before the glue has had time to dry—like real flowers, they will wilt!

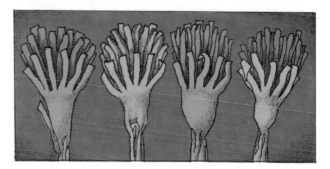

Flower Power

It's not difficult to make flowers out of felt. Felt cuts easily, does not fray at the edges and comes in many different colours. It is also much less floppy than most fabrics.

Give an old skirt or jacket a new lease of life by decorating it with felt flowers.

Choose felt in a colour that goes well with the garment. It's a good idea to draw the outline of the flowers in pencil before you cut them out. Now sew the flowers along the edges or hem of your garment as shown. If you don't like sewing, glue them in place with a special fabric glue.

Any odd flowers left over can be used to decorate a shirt, hat—even a tea cosy! You will probably think up some ideas of your own.

Flower Box

Everyone can find something to put in a box. So a box decorated with felt flowers makes a welcome present.

The box can be either wood or cardboard. Paint it first or, if it's going to be a jewel box, cover it by cutting felt to fit each side and gluing on—inside and out.

Now glue on felt flowers in a toning or contrasting shade. Arrange the flowers on the box and decide on your pattern before you finally stick them down.

Roller Printing

When you have cut out your flowers, you will be left with a piece of felt with flower-shaped holes in it. You can use this to print flowers.

Cut the felt to fit a paint roller and glue it on as shown, making sure it's smoothly stretched with no bumps.

Now put the roller in a tray of paint. The felt should soak up the paint, but the flower shapes—or hollows—should be left clean.

When you roll the roller along a piece of paper, the flowers should appear as pale patches on a coloured background.

Roller print flowers for wall hangings, book covers—or even a frieze along your bedroom walls.

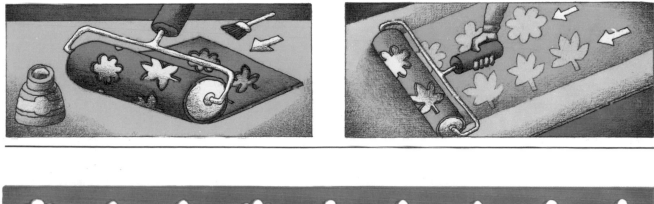

The genie kept on pestering Reginald to tell him his third wish. Perhaps he could teach him a new game to distract him.

'I know, I'll teach you how to play something you never come across in the desert,' he said to the genie. 'Draughts!'

'How many players are there?' asked the genie.

'Only two. One has 12 white draughts and the other 12 black ones.'

'I see—the white draughts go on the white squares and the black on the black ones!'

'No—they all go on the black squares.'

'And each player moves his piece forward, square by square?'

'Yes, but diagonally, not in a straight line. And you can never move them backwards. They move forward, diagonally, until they meet

an enemy piece. If there is an empty square behind it, it can be taken.

'When one of the pieces reaches a square at the other end of the board, it becomes a Queen. Instead of moving just one square at a time, it can now move any number of squares and take any of the enemy pieces that lie in its path—if they have an empty square behind them.'

'I suppose the player with the most Queens is the winner?'

'Not at all. The winner is the one who captures all the other player's draughts.'

'All right. Can you give me any tips?'

'The first rule is never to leave any pieces without protection—with empty spaces behind them.'

'And to take lots of enemy pieces!'

'It's more important to make sure your opponent doesn't take lots of yours. If one of your pieces can take an enemy piece, you must do it, or else your opponent will take your piece in his next go!'

'What happens if no one wins?'

'It's a drawn game.'

'Let's try a game now.'

60

Giant Draughts

Draughts are even more fun if you play with a giant set on a giant board. Play outside, marking out the 64 squares on sand with a stick or on a hard surface (like a playground) with chalk.

For the draughts, use old plates, pot lids, stones, hats, old tyres—anything at all!

61

Meanwhile, Camembert had been trudging through the desert. He was feeling on his last legs when he saw the towers of an oil refinery shining in the distance. When he reached it, he was delighted to find that it was guarded by another mouse.

The mouse told Camembert that the refinery belonged to his boss, Mad O'Hara, who was known as the Oil King.

'Why don't you go and see him? He loves seeing new faces out here!'

So Camembert set off for the Oil King's palace, which the mouse had told him was straight ahead.

Camembert walked on towards the palace. It was an amazing sight, its tower glistening in the sun like spun sugar, and fresh green plants growing round it. At the sight of it Camembert's spirits rose. Surely he would find help here. Unless, of course, it was a mirage?

But the palace wasn't a mirage. And neither was Mad O'Hara, the Oil King, who was delighted to see a new face.

Build an Oil Drilling Tower

To make the tower you need lots of small, flat pieces of wood. Ice lolly sticks are ideal.

You can make really complicated towers, but the simplest kind is the one illustrated opposite.

Join the sticks together, following the illustrations. As they are put together diagonally, it's a good idea to make a drawing first, as shown, so that you can get the correct angles. When they look right, glue them together at the ends. Now build up the tower, following the illustrations.

When you have made the tower, you can go on to make all kinds of other models—from simple cabins or wig-wams to elaborate buildings. For more delicate models, try using spent matchsticks or even wooden cocktail sticks or toothpicks. If you are pleased with your finished model, give it a coat of special enamel model paint.

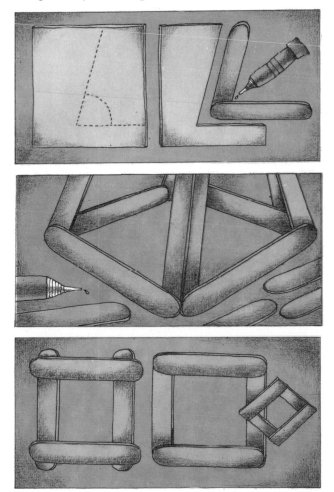

He listened to Camembert's story with many cries of delight and amazement. At the end of it he said, 'I haven't been so amused for a long time! How can I show my thanks? Will you accept a barrel of gold as a gift?'

Camembert explained that he was now stuck in the desert with his friend.

'You live in a big city, don't you?' said Mad O'Hara, 'Well, I have some shopping to do. It's very difficult to get things in the middle of the desert. So I will fly you and your friend home in one of my private planes, if you will spend a morning taking me round the larger stores!'

Camembert agreed at once. But they would have to stop and pick up Reginald. The Oil King was eager to do this, in any case, because he had heard so much about the genie and wanted to see him for himself.

'I hope we spot them,' said Camembert, as they flew off, as slowly as possible.

'What are those strange patterns on the sand?' asked the pilot suddenly.

Looking down below, Camembert saw Reginald's stone patterns—and then Reginald and the genie.

'Good old Reginald!' he said, 'I wouldn't have believed he could have been so clever!'

They landed nearby and rushed over to the pair. Reginald was amazed and delighted, especially when he heard that they were all going to fly home.

'What do you need a plane for?' grumbled the genie. 'I've never been so insulted in my life!'

Before he climbed into the plane, Reginald turned to him and said, 'My last wish. I nearly forgot. I've been so plagued with your dreadful jokes, that I wish you would vanish into a Christmas cracker—and stay there until someone pulls it!'

There was a pop, and they saw a small cracker lying on the sand where the genie had been. 'I expect it will be one of the nomad traders who pulls it,' said Camembert. 'Serve them right!'

As they all flew off towards home, Reginald settled back in his seat, 'Oh, for a quiet life!'